Simon and Molly
plus Hester

Lisa Jahn-Clough

Houghton Mifflin Company Boston 2001
Walter Lorraine Books

Walter Lorraine (wr) Books

All rights reserved. For information about permission
to reproduce selections from this book, write to Permissions,
Houghton Mifflin Company, New York, New York 10003.

www.houghtonmifflinbooks.com

ISBN 0-618-08220-4
Library of Congress No. 2001016851

Printed in the United States of America
PHX 10 9 8 7 6 5 4 3 2 1

Simon and Molly play
together every day.
Just the two of them.

Molly lets Simon ride her two-wheeler.

Simon makes Molly
toast with butter.

They are the best of friends.
Just the two of them.

Until Hester moved in.

"Let's ride the bike," said Simon.
"I don't want to," Hester said.
"Let's make paper airplanes, instead."

"Yay!" said Molly. "I love paper airplanes."
"Not me," said Simon.

The next morning Simon
went to Molly's house.
Hester was there.
"Let's have a snack," Molly said.
Simon made toast with butter.
"Do you have any cinnamon-sugar?"
Hester asked.
"That's a great idea!" said Molly.
Simon ate his toast plain.

"Let's ride the bike," said Simon.
He jumped on the bike so fast that he fell over.
"Are you okay?" Hester asked.
"Leave me alone," said Simon.

That Hester thinks she's so great,
Simon thought. *Molly likes her better than me.*

"Do you want to paint with us?" Molly asked.
"No," said Simon. "I have to go home."

Simon spent all afternoon trying
to make paper airplanes, but none of them worked.
"I wish Hester would fly away," he said.

Simon hid in the tree to watch Molly and Hester.
"Do you want to ride the two-wheeler?"
he heard Molly ask.

"I don't know how," said Hester.
"Really?" Molly asked.
"No one ever taught me," Hester said.

"Simon can teach you," Molly said.
"Do you think so?" Hester asked.
"Simon is the best rider in the
whole world," Molly said.
"And he is my very best friend."

23

I'm her best friend, Simon thought.

"What's this?" Hester asked.
Simon jumped out of the tree.
"It's a paper airplane that doesn't fly," he said.
"Simon!" Molly smiled. "You're here!"
"How about some toast?" Simon asked.
"I'd love some," Molly said.
Simon looked at Hester.

"We can add cinnamon-sugar," Simon said. "Great!" said Hester. "After that, can you teach me how to ride the two-wheeler?" "Okay!" said Simon. "If you show me how to make a paper airplane that flies." "Sure," said Hester.

Now Simon and Molly plus Hester
play together every day.
They ride the two-wheeler.
They eat toast with
cinnamon-sugar.

And they fly paper airplanes.
Just the three of them.

"I'm so glad we're friends," Molly said.
"Me, too," said Simon.
"Me, three," said Hester.